Dedicated to my sweet Audrey …

While I drew the pictures in this book to be especially pleasing to you, it's the story that I want you to remember the most. I hope it will be your first introduction to God's grace, just like it was for me.

And to my daddy, who made the story in the first place.

It was a week before Christmas and Amy and her mommy were visiting some newly born puppies at a friend's house. The puppies were so small and bursting with energy.

One in particular caught Amy's eye: a beautiful, black Yorkshire Terrier who always had its tongue out, ready to kiss at the slightest touch. Amy held it close, even as it squirmed to lick her face, and fell in love.

"If he were mine, I would name him Kisses, because that is what he loves to do," she said.

Amy's mommy loved the puppy too, but knew that Daddy would take more convincing if they wanted to bring the puppy home.

"Daddy, I want a puppy," Amy declared at dinner that night.

"You're too young to have a puppy of your own, honey." Daddy said, as if he had had this conversation hundreds of times before.

"Nu-uh, I would take care of it all by myself. I would Daddy!"

"Mommy and I will talk about it later," he said, and Amy knew not to say anything more. She did, however, look imploringly at her mother, hoping maybe this time her daddy could be convinced.

Later that night when Amy was in bed asleep, her mommy and daddy decided to have a talk. "Maybe it is time to get a puppy, Bill," Amy's mommy said. "They were so cute, I wouldn't mind having one myself!"

"But Amy needs to learn responsibility. If it were to be her puppy, she would have to take care of it. I don't want to always be the one taking it out or feeding it or paying all the vet's bills."

Amy's daddy was trying to teach her how to be a responsible person. He knew this would be an excellent way for her to learn, but he wanted to make sure she would take it seriously.

"Maybe I'll write up a contract that we could have her sign. It could list all the tasks that she would need to do in order to get and keep the puppy."

Amy's mommy looked at him skeptically.

A couple days later, Amy and her parents sat in the family room to talk about the puppy. Amy was so excited she was bursting with smiles. Maybe she would finally get the puppy! Maybe tomorrow she and little Kisses would be playing together on the floor of this very room!

"Amy, I know how much you've been wanting to have a puppy, and your mother and I think you may finally be ready to take care of one. But before you get too excited," Amy's daddy added quickly as he saw his daughter giggling in her chair, "you must agree to some chores that I have already written down. We will talk about them now, and then if you agree, you can sign this paper."

Although she was still excited at the prospect of a new puppy, Amy's smile faded a bit. She was confused by what her daddy was saying to her, but could tell that he was very serious.

"Number one, you must train the dog to only go potty outside and clean up any mistakes he might make around the house. Number two, you must give the dog a bath at least once a week. Number three, you will pay for one half of all doctor's visits including any medication the dog may need."

Amy sat listening as the list went on and on and her heart broke. Her daddy had compiled a list of chores so very long she knew she would never be able to accomplish them all. There was still one hope. If she could just get the puppy in the house, maybe her daddy would forget about the list and allow it to stay anyway. But then her daddy read the last sentence of the contract:

"If Amy is not willing or able to accomplish all the above chores, then the puppy will be sold or given away, and will not be allowed to stay in the house any longer!"

At this, Amy knew her desire would not be fulfilled. She would not get the puppy and Kisses would find a different home. Soon tears flooded her eyes, and she began to cry. Her daddy looked startled, but she managed to explain.

"Daddy," Amy sobbed, with tears pouring down her cheeks, "I can't sign that list. I'd never be able to do all those chores!" With that, she ran out of the room, and headed for her bed.

Amy's mommy and daddy looked at each other. Her daddy looked shocked at his daughter's response.

"I thought for sure she would sign it. I thought she'd sign it without thinking and we'd have to give the puppy away. I thought it would be a valuable tool for teaching responsibility."

"Well, maybe you didn't give your daughter enough credit," said Amy's mommy knowingly as she left to go comfort her daughter.

That night Amy's daddy could not sleep. He kept picturing his little girl crying from something he had done. But the worst part was that he knew she had acted more responsibly than he had given her credit for.

How could he fix this? He wondered.

He wanted so much for his little girl to be happy, but he wanted her to understand his actions. Suddenly, he had an idea. The more he thought about the idea, the more he liked it. But in order for it to work, he had to get up right now and prepare. So he climbed out of bed, and got to work.

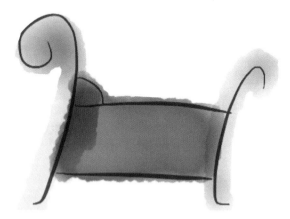

On Christmas Eve, Amy woke up early to a knock on her door.

"Amy, wake up. Daddy wants to show you something," came her mommy's voice from behind the door.

# THE LAW

# Grace

Crawling out of her bed, she took her mommy's hand and was led downstairs to the Christmas tree. Stapled to the wall, Amy recognized the contract her daddy had written, and a sign above it that said, "The Law" in large, bold letters. Next to that was another sign that said, "Grace." Amy looked below the sign and saw a tiny ornament that looked like a puppy. The puppy had a sign on it as well. It said, "Kisses." Amy could feel the excitement coming back, but she was confused.

"What does it mean, Daddy?"

"Come to me," her daddy said, lifting her up to his lap. "Before Jesus came to earth, people who loved Him had to abide by every rule that He asked them to. It was quite clear to the people that they could not keep every single rule. It was just impossible for them. But when Jesus came to earth, everything changed. Because He came and took all of our sins and failures upon Himself, His people won't suffer if they don't follow all the rules. In other words, we now live under grace. Under grace, we love Jesus joyfully, knowing that He freed us from our burdens so that we can enjoy everything He has given to us. That contract I wanted you to sign was like the Law that Jesus gave to his people. It made you cry because you knew you couldn't keep all the rules. But we do not live under the Law anymore. Because of Jesus, we live under grace."

"But daddy, what does it mean to live under grace?" Amy asked.

"It means," her daddy paused and smiled at his daughter. "It means," he said again, "we are getting a puppy."

# *Afterward*

By William E. Barker

I'm the daddy in the story. I'm pretty embarrassed—realizing how silly I was.

Yes, I was trying to instill the kind of discipline in my impressionable little girl that would serve her well in this tough world. But my wife was right, I was going way overboard and I didn't have the good sense to see it, until she (lovingly—well, kind of —but correctly) lectured me based on Colossians 3:21, "Fathers, do not embitter your children, or they will become discouraged." I agreed that I had been too tough, yet I still wanted to use this as an instructional moment. How could I do that now and not discourage Amy?

I went to bed feeling like a pariah, but eventually got to sleep. Then—despite normally being a sound sleeper—I awoke suddenly in the middle of the night with a biblical solution in a biblical wrapper—a gift from God.

The biblical solution was that just as the Law had revealed the distance between humankind and God, my "Puppy Rules" revealed the distance between a well-meaning adult and a young child, as evidenced by my precious daughter's tears. Just as God sent his Son to restore the relationship between humankind and God, I would propose a solution—not requiring that from Amy—thereby restoring the relationship. As I lay in bed, I realized that this is the very picture of justification: God's crediting His people with righteousness through His grace, thereby providing a way that humankind can be restored to God.

I would propose that Amy's mother and I would help her keep the "Puppy Rules"; she wouldn't be very good at keeping the rules at first, and when she failed, we would always forgive her, but as she matured, she would find that keeping the rules was really part of her nature and increasingly easy to do. Still thinking in the dark, I realized that this was a picture of me in my relationship with God and the concept of sanctification: a gradual setting aside of the spiritually immature and becoming more Christlike—complete with failures, but always with forgiveness.

My mind racing now, I thought about how Christ-followers are promised glory for eternity. The Bible calls it glorification. And while a child Amy's age couldn't understand what that means (and really, neither do adults!), she would understand that ultimately all this means is that she would get her puppy—the nicely poignant ending of the story as Amy has recalled it.

These thoughts crystalized, I got up that night long ago, and made the poster board that Amy describes in the story: the Law in the form of "Rules for the Puppy" juxtaposed with a picture of a puppy. But there was a problem (I am a slow learner): how would this simple poster bear the heavy pedagogical burden I had envisioned?

That's when the biblical wrapper came to me in two flashes. The first was that no analogy (and certainly no poster board) could fully capture the ineffably rich subtlety of redemption, and that fact is explicitly discussed and recognized in the Bible. The second flash was to note, with the parables of Jesus in mind, that teachers teach spiritual lessons to students using age-appropriate means, and that's how God teaches His spiritually immature children—whether those children are eight or eighty.

Setting down the tape and the markers, I remembered how in Romans 5-8—a treatise many regard as the definitive statement on redemption—St. Paul uses the theological terms justification, sanctification, and glorification to explain. Yet when he attempts to analogize those lessons, he refers to them in I Corinthians 3:2 simply as "milk" because as he says, the recipients of his letter "were not yet ready for [solid food]". I remembered the writer of Hebrews making a similar point in Hebrews 5:12-13, where someone "not acquainted with the teaching about righteousness" is fed milk, not "solid food". And Peter, in addressing spiritual milk-drinkers, in I Peter 2:2 suggests drinking spiritual milk is the natural and acceptable way to "grow up in [their] salvation".

If Jesus could teach spiritual lessons using the similes of seeds and sheep and the biblical writers could be satisfied with analogies like "milk" and "solid food" when they were referring to great theological truths, could I not use and be satisfied with just two poster panels: the "Puppy Rules" on one side and a picture of the puppy on the other?

That I needed such a revelation after the events of the day before is still a source of embarrassment!

I returned to bed and slept soundly since the biblical lesson in its biblical wrapper was complete, in the form of a simple poster board.

Well, not quite. Years ago, when Amy first posted this story on her blog, some commenters criticized her for using such a simple analogy to capture the profound truth of redemption. I came to her defense by saying that it seemed pedantic to base criticisms of Amy's story on the fact that analogies are flawed or incomplete. Of course they are, I said, but explaining profound concepts gradually, starting with simple and moving to more complete explanations once the immature had matured, is a method that biblical writers seem to condone and encourage.

Today I would suggest that Amy's capturing this story explicitly so she can teach her own children validates the use of analogies compellingly well. Having over time learned deeply the profound truths of redemption, she now wants to pass them along to her children, using a simple story. This too is a biblical wrapper.

And there is still another, as I think about it now: just as our Father in Heaven sometimes gives us "immeasurably more than all we ask or imagine" (Ephesians 3:20), it's worth noting that in fact, Amy grew up with not one, but two little puppies—one named Hugs and the other Kisses—because, you see, when Amy and her parents got to the kennel to pick up her puppy, the daddy suggested they get two.

Made in the USA
Charleston, SC
16 November 2015